PRAISE FOR M. L.

A fabulous soaring thriller.

— *TAKE OVER AT MIDNIGHT,* MIDWEST
BOOK REVIEW

Meticulously researched, hard-hitting, and suspenseful.

— *PURE HEAT,* PUBLISHERS WEEKLY,
STARRED REVIEW

Expert technical details abound, as do realistic military missions with superb imagery that will have readers feeling as if they are right there in the midst and on the edges of their seats.

— *LIGHT UP THE NIGHT,* RT REVIEWS, 4
1/2 STARS

Buchman has catapulted his way to the top tier of my favorite authors.

— FRESH FICTION

Nonstop action that will keep readers on the edge of their seats.

— *TAKE OVER AT MIDNIGHT,* LIBRARY JOURNAL

M L. Buchman's ability to keep the reader right in the middle of the action is amazing.

— LONG AND SHORT REVIEWS

The only thing you'll ask yourself is, "When does the next one come out?"

— *WAIT UNTIL MIDNIGHT,* RT REVIEWS, 4 STARS

The first...of (a) stellar, long-running (military) romantic suspense series.

— *THE NIGHT IS MINE,* BOOKLIST, "THE 20 BEST ROMANTIC SUSPENSE NOVELS: MODERN MASTERPIECES"

I knew the books would be good, but I didn't realize how good.

— NIGHT STALKERS SERIES, KIRKUS REVIEWS

Buchman mixes adrenalin-spiking battles and brusque military jargon with a sensitive approach.

— PUBLISHERS WEEKLY

13 times "Top Pick of the Month"

— NIGHT OWL REVIEWS

Tom Clancy fans open to a strong female lead will clamor for more.

— *DRONE*, PUBLISHERS WEEKLY

Superb! Miranda is utterly compelling!

— *BOOKLIST,* STARRED REVIEW

Miranda Chase continues to astound and charm.

— BARB M.

Escape Rating: A. Five Stars! OMG just start with *Drone* and be prepared for a fantastic binge-read!

— READING REALITY

The best military thriller I've read in a very long time. Love the female characters.

BLACK BOX

A MIRANDA CHASE TEAM STORY

M. L. BUCHMAN

Receive a free book and discover more by this author at: www. mlbuchman.com

Cover images:

Wallpaper 180 © DJAndyW

MD Helicopter 902 Explorer © Luc Williams

SIGN UP FOR M. L. BUCHMAN'S NEWSLETTER TODAY

Other works by M. L. Buchman: *(* - also in audio)*

Action-Adventure Thrillers

Dead Chef
One Chef!
Two Chef!

Miranda Chase
*Drone**
*Thunderbolt**
*Condor**
*Ghostrider**
*Raider**
*Chinook**
*Havoc**
*White Top**
*Start the Chase**

Science Fiction / Fantasy

Deities Anonymous
Cookbook from Hell: Reheated
Saviors 101

Single Titles
Monk's Maze
the Me and Elsie Chronicles

Contemporary Romance

Eagle Cove
Return to Eagle Cove
Recipe for Eagle Cove
Longing for Eagle Cove
Keepsake for Eagle Cove

Love Abroad
Heart of the Cotswolds: England
Path of Love: Cinque Terre, Italy

Where Dreams
Where Dreams are Born
Where Dreams Reside
*Where Dreams Are of Christmas**
Where Dreams Unfold
Where Dreams Are Written
Where Dreams Continue

Non-Fiction

Strategies for Success
Managing Your Inner Artist/Writer
*Estate Planning for Authors**
Character Voice
Narrate and Record Your Own
*Audiobook**

Short Story Series by M. L. Buchman:

Action-Adventure Thrillers

Dead Chef

Miranda Chase Origin Stories

Romantic Suspense

Antarctic Ice Fliers

US Coast Guard

Contemporary Romance

Eagle Cove

Other

Deities Anonymous (fantasy)

Single Titles

The Emily Beale Universe
(military romantic suspense)

The Night Stalkers
MAIN FLIGHT
The Night Is Mine
I Own the Dawn
Wait Until Dark
Take Over at Midnight
Light Up the Night
Bring On the Dusk
By Break of Day
Target of the Heart
Target Lock on Love
Target of Mine
Target of One's Own
NIGHT STALKERS HOLIDAYS
Daniel's Christmas *
Frank's Independence Day *
Peter's Christmas *
Christmas at Steel Beach
Zachary's Christmas *
Roy's Independence Day *
Damien's Christmas *
Christmas at Peleliu Cove

Henderson's Ranch
Nathan's Big Sky *
Big Sky, Loyal Heart *
Big Sky Dog Whisperer *
Tales of Henderson's Ranch *

Shadow Force: Psi
At the Slightest Sound *
At the Quietest Word *
At the Merest Glance *
At the Clearest Sensation *

White House Protection Force
Off the Leash *
On Your Mark *
In the Weeds *

Firehawks
Pure Heat
Full Blaze
Hot Point *
Flash of Fire *
Wild Fire
SMOKEJUMPERS
Wildfire at Dawn *
Wildfire at Larch Creek *
Wildfire on the Skagit *

Delta Force
Target Engaged *
Heart Strike *
Wild Justice *
Midnight Trust *

Emily Beale Universe Short Story Series

The Night Stalkers
The Night Stalkers Stories
The Night Stalkers CSAR
The Night Stalkers Wedding Stories
The Future Night Stalkers

Delta Force
Th Delta Force Shooters
The Delta Force Warriors

Firehawks
The Firehawks Lookouts
The Firehawks Hotshots
The Firebirds

White House Protection Force
Stories

Future Night Stalkers
Stories (Science Fiction)

ABOUT THIS BOOK

WHEN IT'S TIME TO LEAVE THE TEAM, CAN THEY ACTUALLY GO?

Jeremy's skills make him ready to leave Miranda's aircrash investigation team and start his own. But neither Jeremy nor Miranda are prepared for it when the time comes.

Jeremy must take the lead. Miranda must stay behind. The change forces each member of the team to grapple with their own challenges.

Does the answer lie in the black box of a flight data recorder? Maybe it does.

1

"THIS IS REALLY SAD." JEREMY STARED AT THE READOUT ON the computer screen. Was so aware of the feel of the keyboard that it hurt his fingertips.

"What is? The pilot? The FAA who issued his med card. Not us."

He and Holly were the only two here tonight. Without the other four team members present, the secure office Miranda had built in the back of an aircraft hangar for her air-crash investigation team was echoing in the evening quiet. The sun had disappeared behind the towering Olympic Mountains hours ago, and now the sky darkened with true sunset. Beyond the two big windows, the runway lights at Tacoma Narrows Airport had flickered on but it was a small airport and boasted little traffic after dark.

"I wasn't talking about him. I was talking about this." He rested a hand on the bright orange flight data recorder. "This is the last Black Box I'll ever read for Miranda." He knew it was stupid, and Holly would laugh if he did, but he wanted to stroke the battered casing like it was a puppy dog.

All flight recorders were supposed to be sent to the National Transportation Board's lab for examination. But no one had dared argue with Miranda when she'd purchased a Black Box reader for the team. He still sent the badly damaged ones back to the NTSB labs because they had recovery equipment he didn't, but Miranda's cases often couldn't afford the time to ship the recorder to Washington, DC for analysis.

"Last one? You're done then? Good! You're always underfoot, mate, and we're all glad to be rid of you." After two years of working together, he didn't need to hear Holly's light Australian accent shift to Broad Strine to know she was joking.

"Won't miss you more than dingo's breath, *mate,*" he muttered back.

Holly burst out laughing and gave him a one-armed hug. "Your accent sucks, but you're learning, my young Padawan."

"God, there are so many things I'm going to miss." It was like someone was ripping out his insides.

"Including me?"

"Maybe not *you* so much," but they shared smiles that belied his statement.

"You know it's the right step? You do get that, don't you, Jeremy?" A serious Holly was unusual enough to garner his full attention. He half-turned to look at her. Tall, blonde, beautiful, and generally scary as hell. She looked a little worried and her accent had gone the way dingo breaths hopefully went—away.

"I guess."

Holly smacked him lightly on the side of the head as if he really was her kid brother. "Senior member of the Analysis Lab for the NTSB at the Washington, DC, headquarters? At twenty-seven years old no less. And you and your girlfriend both as consultants to the US Air Force Accident Investigation Board. Tell me how you could land in any sweeter spot."

He couldn't, so he didn't try. But he didn't have to be a genius to know that no matter what else happened, two years on Miranda's team would be one of his life's highlights.

How many airplane crashes had he studied with her, both in the field and hunched over this bench? The jump from new graduate of the NTSB Academy to the absolute top team had been a miracle. No one was as good as Miranda.

Jeremy turned back to the computer screen. There had been no surprises here. The brand-new Cessna 408 SkyCourier turboprop freighter had been type-certified for just one month, and now they'd had their first full hull-loss incident. A bird strike in the Number Two engine had certainly wounded the aircraft but it had been designed to survive that. At least until the delivery pilot had a heart attack several seconds later.

No, that was a postulation.

Yes, the coroner had identified a massive coronary. And, yes, the cockpit voice recorder had captured a series of sounds immediately after the bird strike that would be commensurate with a major attack.

Bad one, mate. That must hurt worse than a hornets' nest

down your drawers, Holly had commented when they'd listened to the recordings. She'd been the only one around to serve as a second listener.

So, not conclusive, but very highly indicative.

He finished the initial findings report and prepared to send it to Miranda for review.

"You're a full investigator now, Jeremy." Holly nudged him before he could he send it.

He was. The new ID badge tucked into his vest pocket declared he was qualified to be an Investigator-in-charge. And this had been his site investigation at Boeing Field while the others were busy conducting a training. Except for his girlfriend. Taz was busy packing up their own few belongings for the upcoming move.

Moving the cursor from Report Preparation to Investigator, he typed in his name, attached his transcription of the recording, and sent it to the NTSB. Who knew? Maybe next week he'd be the investigator in DC leading this report review.

He unplugged the data cables from the Black Box recorder and shut down his computer. Holly helped him package the recorder for FedEx pickup.

Finally, he gathered up the Black Box interface cables, outboard format converters, and the removable drive they kept the specialized software on. Rather than tucking it in his site pack, he carried it over to Miranda's rolltop desk and locked it in the small safe she used as a footrest.

Leaving another piece of himself behind.

Worse, it would shift another burden over to Miranda. She was the only one on the team who understood the proper way to use it. There would be no one to handle it for her once he was gone.

He dropped down onto one of the couches.

"Oh gods, Holly. What have I done?" He hid his face in his hands because he didn't want her to see him cry.

"Do you really want to know?" She sat beside him, but didn't wrap an arm around him, not that he'd expect something like that from her.

He shook his head, "But tell me anyway."

"You grew up, young Padawan."

"I'll try to cut down on that in the future."

Instead of laughing, Holly was quiet for a long time before she whispered, "When you figure out how, let me know."

He looked up at her, but she was studying the darkness outside the office windows.

2

"YOU'RE MISERABLE."

Miranda wished she could argue the point. Her own feelings were often as much a mystery to herself as they were to others—one of the many joys of living a life on the autism spectrum. Still, this time she couldn't doubt that Andi's assessment landed exactly on point.

She sat in her favorite corner on her favorite couch under her favorite quilt but still didn't feel comforted.

As soon as their training was done, she and Andi had flown up to her island. They'd eaten a quiet meal together, showered...but she'd known there was no rest in her bed. Instead she'd come here to the big upstairs sitting room that faced the panoramic view to the south. Even at night, the stars above the silhouette outlines of San Juan, Shaw, and Orcas Islands were breathtaking. This had been her favorite place in the house since she'd first figured out how to crawl out of her crib.

Andi had followed her. Perhaps she couldn't sleep either. She sat at the far end of the couch.

Miranda's head was spinning. "Three weeks. How did so much change in three weeks? I don't know if I can do this. Jeremy and Taz leaving. All of the media that still want to talk to me about the Vice President's crash investigation. All—" She shuddered. An unfinished sentence just another pinch on her soul but she couldn't continue.

"Three weeks?" Then Andi whooshed as if someone had punched her in the stomach. There was only the two of them on the whole island, if Miranda didn't count the sheep and deer and so on. Several of them had tried to butt Andi, though only when she was walking with Miranda. Andi claimed they were jealous. However, they were all outside so it seemed unlikely that any had just headbutted Andi here inside however much it sounded as if one had.

"What?"

"Am... *I* one of those things that's too much change?"

Miranda considered. The few people she'd ever dated before had been men. Her relationship with Andi had indeed also begun three weeks ago.

Andi was...

"You're both easier and harder."

"How so?"

"That. Right there," Miranda pointed at her. Then she realized that both of her hands were under the quilt so that only she herself knew where she was pointing. Unsure if that invalidated the positional indicator, she pulled out her hand to where they could both see it and pointed again.

"My breasts? I barely have any." Andi looked down at

her chest. She was a slim Chinese woman who looked fine to Miranda. Redirecting her finger direction to indicate Andi's head didn't achieve what she intended to indicate either. She closed her hand and tucked it back under the quilt where she apparently should have left it in the first place.

"That," she said for lack of any precise indicator. "The men I've dated in the past would rarely—" *never* seemed closer to the truth than *rarely,* but wasn't wholly accurate, "—ask a question about my feelings. They would be offended or angry or amused or I don't understand what by any response I gave. You ask—and then you listen. That is quantifiably easier as it provides a forum for a more accurate consensus of understanding. Yet, curiously, it also makes you more difficult because I'm forced to clarify my thinking in ways that I hadn't previously, well, thought of thinking about thinking."

"I'm not sure that answers the question."

Miranda had learned when running investigation trainings that a demonstration often far outweighed any explanation she could make. Perhaps that was also true when personal feelings were involved.

To test that hypothesis, she lifted the side of the quilt and gestured for Andi to come join her under it. She smiled happily and within moments they were pressed firmly hip-to-hip and shoulder-to-shoulder. Andi never failed to recall that Miranda didn't enjoy light contact. They arranged the quilt over them before much of the warmth had escaped.

Her demonstration hypothesis was valid through a

single iteration. She would watch for future opportunities to test and further validate, or invalidate, the result.

"I suppose this means that we, as a couple, aren't the part that is too much change?" Andi asked.

"No. Simply easier and harder. I do come here to the island to decompress from excessive social interaction mandated by my job. But surprisingly you don't appear to interfere with that."

"Good. I'm glad. If you ever *do* need to be alone, simply tell me. If you tell me first, then I'll know not to be offended. Or I'll try."

Miranda decided this wasn't the opportune moment to quote Yoda's philosophy about trying versus doing.

Andi leaned forward enough to let a waft of the Spring air coming in through the open window overlooking the island's darkness slip in. She tucked the quilt more completely around both of their legs and then returned to her former position.

Miranda had been enjoying the feel of the cool air on her feet but it might be rude to complain so she made no mention.

"The real problem is Jeremy and Taz leaving, isn't it?"

Miranda tried to say that wasn't a problem. Her attempt to emote that it was a wonderful opportunity for Jeremy and for Taz as well, wouldn't materialize. Colonel Taz Cortez would be returning to the Pentagon where she'd spent nineteen years—over half her life. She'd have a new role there, this time with the Accident Investigation Board, but it was a world she knew well. Well enough to protect Jeremy? How was Miranda supposed to know?

Andi rested her head on Miranda's shoulder. Her hair

was always thick and smooth. It was like a wash of cool water against her cheek, as if rinsing her face in a pure mountain stream. A nice metaphor. At least she hoped it was because metaphors were still elusive and she was happy with this one. She kept it to herself because she didn't want to know if she was wrong.

They sat together under the quilt. Miranda enjoyed the warmth of companionship and the cool slickness of Andi's hair so much thicker than her own.

Jeremy is leaving. She tried the thought. It still was neither confident nor comfortable, which failed to jibe properly with her certain knowledge that it was the correct action for him.

Leaving? She hadn't really thought about that aspect of it. His not being here anymore, yes, but his actual departure? No.

"My mother taught me that when someone is leaving, you should throw them a going-away party."

"That's a great idea, Miranda. We should have it here. On the island."

"What do you do for a going-away party?" Her mother hadn't lived long enough to teach her that.

"Well, we could get him presents for his new place in DC. And have a cake and a meal."

"A cake and a meal? Is it traditional for the cake to come first in a going-away party? Why do they invert the order or—"

"It's just the order I said it in, Miranda. We'd probably have the cake second."

"What if there are two courses?"

"I'll make sure that it's served last."

"Oh good. That way I won't have to worry about it until the very end. Thank you, Andi."

"Anything for you, Miranda."

Quite why Andi said it with a breathy undertone close by her ear, Miranda didn't know. She pulled the quilt tight under her chin, which re-exposed her feet to the pleasantly cool air, and let herself lean against Andi and slide toward sleep.

3

"WHAT THE HELL IS THAT?"

Jeremy followed Taz's irritated tone. An absolute morning person, within a minute of waking up she was dressed and ready for the day. He tried to keep up but hadn't succeeded once in their nine months together.

She stood in the living room of the team house beside a neat stack of moving boxes. While he and Holly had been finishing the SkyCourier report, Taz had reduced their belongings into such a small space that it would fit in his Prius hybrid without having to mail a single box ahead. He and Taz were so rarely apart that they hadn't missed her sagging Toyota Corolla when it had finally collapsed.

He couldn't believe that he'd soon be living with her.

That wasn't precisely accurate, as they'd been sleeping together ever since she'd joined the team nine months ago. But they'd been doing it in the team house with Mike and Holly. Andi, too, until recently when she'd started spending so much time up on Miranda's private

Spieden Island up in the San Juans. He still wasn't used to that change.

But by this time next week, he and Taz would be living together *in their own place.* Two trips to DC for meetings, and a whirlwind tour with a real estate agent, had landed them a townhouse condo there.

Of course, this stack of boxes would seem even smaller when moved into an empty condo. But Taz wasn't looking at them. She was standing at the window that faced the driveway with her arms crossed tightly in front of her.

He stepped up behind her, slipped his hands around her waist, and rested his chin on top of her head. Mike and Holly must still be asleep. Jeremy decided that maybe he liked the idea of it being only the two of them sometimes.

Though he could *feel* her glaring.

"What the heck is what?" It was crazy, but every time he touched her, his world went quiet. It was like the world only made sense when—

"That!" she jabbed a finger toward the driveway.

A twenty-four-foot IKEA truck was backing in.

"I don't know. Maybe it's a delivery truck?"

Taz growled. It was a deep growl completely incongruous on the petite four-foot-eleven Latina. "Why is it coming here?"

He shrugged, which was a mistake. The motion gave her enough freedom to stride out of his arms.

He followed her out the door. The smooth pea gravel of the front path tickled his bare feet as it slid underfoot.

Taz had her usual hiking boots on already. She was always prepared to move fast.

The delivery driver climbed down. "Go a load here for a Miranda Chase."

"Oh," Taz signed for it. "Jeremy get the garage door. I guess they don't deliver to the island."

"Right." He stepped off the path and onto the driveway. The heavier crushed stone was sharp and had him mincing over to the paved lip of the garage door. Next time he'd remember—shoes first. No, he wouldn't remember, but it was nice to think that he would.

The garage had only two bays. One was for Holly's Corvette. Mike's Mazda Miata was parked next to his own Prius to the side of the house. They always left an open garage bay for the nights Miranda stayed here—which wasn't very often. In most of her aircraft, her island, at ninety miles away, was under half an hour flight. In her Sabrejet it was a mere ten minutes.

The driver didn't pull out a box, he began tugging a tower of boxes onto the liftgate with a pallet jack.

"What's she going to do with all of that?" Her big house on the island, a former resort, had always seemed comfortably furnished to him.

Conversation was briefly impossible as the liftgate lowered and grounded out on the gravel with a loud whine then a crunch.

"The pallet behind this is hers as well," the driver slid the first one into the garage.

Jeremy wondered if she'd bought another house? But that made no sense. The team house had three bedrooms and it was fully furnished. Besides, with his and Taz's departure, the team was shrinking, not growing.

At least he hadn't heard of anyone replacing him. Yet. Knowing it was inevitable didn't make him like it any better.

He looked north. Her own house was elegantly furnished, including a number of antiques that her mother had favored.

He looked to the west into the living room window as the driver was tucking the second pallet beside the first in the garage. This team house was already furnished with IKEA furniture.

Then south toward where toward the hangar office five miles away. She'd furnished that with IKEA deliveries as well.

Finally he looked to the east, *far* to the east, and he knew.

"We're going to need a truck."

Taz looked at him in surprise. "Why?"

"Oh good. It arrived." Miranda and Andi had pulled up on the other side of the IKEA truck in her Porsche Taycan electric sports sedan. She had let him drive it several times. They had discussed the electric- versus gasoline-powered torque coefficients at length. That had led them to meetings with several electric airplane developers. Personally, he'd love to own a Sun Flyer from Aero Electric, but he wasn't a pilot and had just bought a house. Maybe someday he'd have an electric plane.

"What's all this?" Andi asked.

"I couldn't sleep last night. And—"

Jeremy wrapped her in a hug and the rest of her

sentence was muffled against his shoulder, further drowned by the truck's departure.

He wouldn't think to hug his team leader. But hugging Miranda in thanks he could do without feeling too weird. Maybe not if he'd thought about it first, but he hadn't, so he had.

"Why do we need a truck?" Taz asked again.

"But you fell asleep with me..." Andi started, then stopped herself. She looked confused and hurt.

Miranda moved out of the hug as soon as Jeremy released her and went to inspect the boxes. Andi tagged along but didn't say a word as Miranda appeared to be reviewing some mental checklist.

"I downloaded the floor plan of your condo from the real estate site. I thought this would give you a good start in your new home. It should look nice."

"I'm sure it will," Jeremy knew that Miranda had impeccable taste.

"A truck for..." Taz's voice trailed off as she finally caught up with what was happening.

She was usually so quick that it was rare for Jeremy to reach a conclusion before she did—but he had this time. He tried not to feel smug about it but failed miserably.

"Well, starve the lizards. Some chap has made quite the haul." Holly came out of the house and was blinking at the pile of boxes. She wore nothing but a women's soccer t-shirt and gym shorts that were very strong on the *short* part. Mike followed close behind; they were both carrying coffee cups practically the size of their heads.

That's when he spotted the look on Taz's face and knew trouble was brewing.

Jeremy moved to find out what was wrong, but Taz turned toward Miranda. A light touch on Miranda's arm had her twisting to look at Taz. Miranda hated light touches.

"Sorry," Taz managed a rough whisper as she snatched her hand away. "You furnished our...*home?*" The last word barely managed to stumble out of her.

"Yes. I wanted you to be comfortable in your new home. I considered having it delivered and pre-assembled for you in Washington, DC, but that seemed presumptuous. Would that have been presumptuous? I didn't want to wake you last night to ask, so I had them deliver it here. I also acquired most of a kitchen, though I did text Holly. She and Mike are buying you a professional coffee and espresso machine."

"It should be here later today," Mike filled in. "I didn't let *her* pick it out."

"Me and kitchens, mate. Strictly hands off." They shared a happy smile and shifted onto a sunlit patch of the grass to enjoy the morning's warmth as they sipped their coffee.

"Miranda, that was amazingly considerate of you." Jeremy told her as he knew that Miranda had no way to judge such things.

She turned to look at Andi who nodded in agreement.

"Good," Miranda turned back to Taz.

However, Taz's reaction was not at all what Jeremy had expected.

She had stood still through the whole interchange as if frozen in place. Then she began to cry.

He'd never seen Taz cry.

She wrapped Miranda in a hard hug.

"You smell salty," Miranda commented as Taz's damp cheeks pressed against Miranda's chin.

"Yeah," Taz managed on a low gasp of breath, "I do."

Miranda patted Taz on the back a couple of times.

When Miranda turned and looked at him and Andi for what to do next, the only thing either of them could do was shrug. He might be sleeping with Taz, but that didn't mean he understood her.

4

"I don't know what came over me."

Jeremy had chased Taz down to the waterfront. Well, he'd tried to, but by his third step on the driveway, it hurt his feet too much. Yet by the time he could go inside to get shoes, he'd have lost her. So he hobbled over to the grass, raced along the cool blades that soothed his itchy feet, until he reached the sidewalk. There he broke into a run, still wincing at the occasional pebble or twig.

She was quick, but he hoped his guess of where she was heading would pay off.

Sure enough, he caught up with her at the waterside lookout a mere two blocks from the house. A wooden deck with a few benches, it had become one of their favorite evening hangout spots. Especially when everyone was at the house and they needed to get away. Taz had more trouble with crowds than he did, which was odd because she was so much better with people.

He moved to the outermost bench, close by the railing, and sat beside her.

The sun was rising over the Cascades and pouring across Puget Sound. The town of Gig Harbor wrapped around a well-protected bay also called Gig Harbor. A mile long and a quarter-mile wide, they now sat at the very head of it. The harbor was thick with pleasure boats and liveaboards making it postcard-level picturesque against the backdrop of towering Douglas firs and the mountains beyond.

Jeremy would miss living here. Trading the Pacific Northwest for suburban DC. He still wasn't sure about that. Taz had found them a nice place along the Anacostia River. It was also close by the Arboretum, which was a great spot for her to run in.

Probably more so than here.

"I really don't know," Taz repeated herself.

He'd learned to respect her hair-trigger reflexes. But she appeared calm enough now for him to slip his arm around her and tug her to lean against him.

"Seriously. What?" she asked without turning from the view.

He'd rather been hoping that she'd tell *him*. Reading a Black Box was far easier than reading what was going on in his lover's mind.

"Maybe…" he tried tentatively but didn't find any words that wanted to follow that first one.

"Yes?"

"You know…" He remembered the flight curves on the investigation that he and Holly had been working on late into last night. "When a plane is in normal flight, the Black Box recordings are the most tedious thing there is to review. Smooth flight, perhaps some turbulence. Hours of nothing. So much nothing that most Black Boxes write over themselves every two hours. Nothing of interest… until something major happens. Then all hell breaks loose."

"Like me crying for the first time since I was a little girl."

"Right, like that. The first time? Really?"

She nodded as she hung her head. "Everything was going so good. Or I thought it was. And then suddenly I was a weeping like an I-don't-know what."

The chaos of Taz's life, if he were to graph it out—with the murder of her father, the horrible price she'd had to pay to cross the border from Mexico at eleven, her mother's death, and all of the ups and downs of her military career including multiple near-death experiences—would look more like the failure-and-crash lines on a flight record.

In fact…

He started to laugh.

Taz twisted out from under his arm to glare at him, but he couldn't stop it.

"Jer-e-my," she drew it out like a threat.

He dragged her in and kissed the tip of her nose.

"The joke is, that for the first time in your life you actually *are* in smooth flight. Your Black Box record to date would make an airplane crash look good. More than that. For maybe the first time, you're in a clean climb. You were given a full pardon, your rank and pension were reinstated, you were given back your respect. The one thing you've always dreamed of—a home—is actually coming true. I'll bet that was a heck of a jolt to your system. For maybe the first time in your life, you're going to have a real home."

"A *real* home?" Her tone was...thoughtful? Wistful? Surprised?

"Yes. You and me. We're going to have a home that's yours. Ours. When was the last time you had a home that wasn't base housing or some crap temporary apartment?"

"Never. Literally never. The Mexico City and San Diego barrios definitely don't count."

"Always surprising when a dream comes true, isn't it?" He kissed her temple as she settled once more inside the curve of his arm.

What was that like? Ever since learning about Miranda Chase, his sole dream had been to meet her someday. Instead of meeting her at some NTSB training, he'd spent two years working with her. Now *that* was dream fulfillment.

Other dreams? He was sure he had some.

He'd always kind of hoped to meet a woman to be with, someday. Though he'd never pictured anyone like the fireball Colonel Taz Cortez, she was also more wonderful than he'd ever imagined he'd find. But it hadn't been a consuming dream until after it was already happening.

But what did he dream of now?

As he and Taz sat watching the on-going daybreak, he couldn't come up with a single idea. Whatever it might be lay hidden in some Black Box.

5

ANDI FLEW THEM ALL UP TO THE ISLAND TOGETHER IN Miranda's MD 902N Explorer helicopter. Miranda flew in the front right-hand seat, which was very disorienting.

In an airplane, the left seat was the pilot's. In a helicopter, it was the right seat. Except she wasn't much of a helicopter pilot yet. Andi still always rode the controls with her.

That was another thing that had changed in the last three weeks. She'd never flown a helicopter at all three weeks ago. Andi had been giving her flying lessons since, but it still felt wrong. She recalled the transition from tricycle to bicycle. All inherent stability had been lost and she'd carried the bruises to prove it for weeks. She still didn't enjoy bicycles to this day.

A helicopter was like that, able to move in all three dimensions, often simultaneously. Plus pitch, roll, and yaw. The last was especially disconcerting. Andi had demonstrated that it was possible to spin around completely while still flying at a constant speed on a fixed heading. Miranda barely felt comfortable with straight-and-level flight. Though gentle turns were no longer terrifying, now merely harrowing.

"Bank right." Andi called out over the cockpit intercom. The others in the back were on a different circuit so that they wouldn't distract her.

"But Spieden Island is straight ahead."

"There's something I want to see from the air."

Miranda banked right. She always flew the most efficient course between two points. Andi kept her turning until they were on an 030 heading.

"Next time, ease up on the collective a little more during a turn to maintain your altitude through the turn."

Miranda inspected the instruments; she'd lost almost fifty feet. That was unacceptable. She began to correct her altitude by easing back on the cyclic.

But the cyclic wouldn't move. She pulled harder; it was still frozen in place.

Had the helicopter broken? Had some locking mechanism clicked into place without her noticing? Was it— She turned to Andi, and saw her smile. Her right hand was clenched tightly around her own cyclic joystick, resisting Miranda's motion.

Then she knew why and felt foolish. "Oh, right. A small correction like that in an airplane is done with the control yoke. But in a helicopter, applying additional lift with the *collective* controls the altitude."

She eased up on the collective with her left hand until they were once more exactly at fifteen hundred feet. The cyclic came free as Andi returned to simply riding her hands on the controls.

"I guess we're going this way."

"I guess we are," Andi agreed over the intercom. "Now watch out for air traffic, it's going to become heavy and erratic up ahead."

Miranda searched the skies and spotted several glints of mid-morning sunlight shining off aircraft hulls. They were circling like…birds of prey over a carcass.

"What died down there?"

Andi laughed. It was a bright, merry sound that was one of Miranda's favorite things about her. Andi flicked over to the full intercom.

"Folks, get out your cameras. We're about to fly over the famous tulip fields of La Conner, Washington. They're past peak, but they were very late this year, so I'll bet they're still amazing."

And sure enough, there they were. Great bands of color like someone had spraypainted the fields in great long stripes of purple, yellow, white, and red. Some strips were pink, others maroon, and a few looked like they'd been painted with a spattering brush where all of the colors were mixed together.

She checked the air traffic, most of which was following a lazy clockwise spiral. It was by far the most common landing pattern, so it made sense that most pilots would automatically select that. A part of her wanted to go counterclockwise. To be a contrarian? Or perhaps she was finally owning that her Spectrum Disorder would keep her from belonging in *any* group.

Yet she belonged in this group, with these five people.

And two of them were leaving.

A pilot didn't arbitrarily relinquish the controls. She was still emotionally competent and therefore retained command and began to follow in the neat circles other pilots had adopted.

She was too old for tantrums—but she could wish that she wasn't.

6

"You two go walkabout," Holly practically shoved them out the door of Miranda's house.

"But I want to make—"

"Shush!"

Jeremy shrugged on the vest he didn't need on this warm afternoon but Holly had shoved into his hands. She leaned in, whispered into Miranda's ear, then closed the door in Miranda's face.

"What did she say?"

"She said that she, Mike, and Taz would bake your cake and we should get out of the way because it's a surprise."

"Not anymore."

Miranda squinted at him for a moment, then sighed. "I guess not. I was never good at keeping secrets."

"No, you aren't." Experience had taught Jeremy that. Unless it had to do with a security clearance, then she was as secure as a Swiss vault. "So where shall we go?"

"My island is less than three miles long and a half-mile wide. I've never measured the exact circumference, especially not including the crenulations of shoreline at various tidal levels. But it doesn't strike me as a sufficient space for an Australian walkabout as practiced by their Aboriginal First Peoples. A proper coming-of-age walkabout traditionally spans six months and may cover a thousand miles. I've never tried to make a hundred and ninety laps of my island."

"I don't think she intended us to spend the next six months circling the island. I think that a stroll through the woods or along the shore would be sufficient." Jeremy turned his back on the house and they began walking around the perimeter of the vegetable garden, toward the tall Douglas fir woods at the north end of the island.

He could see Miranda still puzzling at it as they walked. "I think she merely wanted you to get me out of the way for a while so that I would be surprised by the cake."

"Oh," Miranda nodded. "I understand now. Her use of hyperbole does seem rather extreme though, don't you think?"

"It's Holly."

"Yes, she is rather random at times." Miranda gasped and spun to face the house. "My kitchen. She's going to make a complete mess of my kitchen. Everything from flour to measuring spoons will be all higgledy-piggledy."

"Yep," Jeremy took her arm, tucked it around his elbow, and led her away from the house. Nothing either of them could do would ever stop, or change, Holly.

They walked in silence along the top of the island. It was little more than a long ridge humped up out of the depths of Puget Sound. The terrain was divided neatly down its entire length, with lush meadows to the west and thick trees to the east. The single dirt road ran from the boathouse at the southern cove past the house at one third of the island's length and the airplane hangar beside the ridge-top grass landing strip at two-thirds.

Everything felt different. Not bad, but different.

Somehow, he was being the adult rather than simply following in Miranda's footsteps. She was twelve years older and he'd never be as good as her but he felt somehow...taller. At five-seven that might not be saying much, but it was true.

Miranda stopped to greet one of the sika deer that wandered the island. Spieden had briefly been a shooting-safari resort, stocked with wild animals for that purpose. Most had been rescued, but Japanese sika deer, big-horned Caspian Mouflon sheep, and an amazing variety of ground birds still wandered the island. With no natural predators, they all seemed to think Miranda was simply one of them. Or perhaps their mom.

She greeted several by name and even made admiring noises about the spring fawns to several of the mother deer. "I'm so sorry. They pushed me out of the house so fast, that I didn't have time to grab any dried apples. Come to the house later."

The funny thing was that they usually did. If the rest of the team was inside, a couple of them would come nosing around in the evenings. Only Miranda didn't spook them. At the moment, he must be in some sort of Miranda bubble. They didn't approach him, but they didn't particularly shy away. Maybe they were more confident here in the woods.

Could he be more confident outside of his environment, Miranda's team?

He would have to be. Of course, he'd been trained by the best there was. He liked the sound of that.

"Go play. Go play." Miranda shooed the deer away and they wandered out across the meadow to graze.

He didn't know what to say to her as they continued on their way. The soft rustle of grass in the morning breeze to either side of the road faded as they reached the grass runway. Miranda kept it mowed as neatly as a golf fairway.

"I, uh, put the Black Box reader in the safe under your desk."

They were past the hangar which had her two jets and her helicopter tucked inside before she responded.

"No. I think you should take it with you."

"But what will you use?"

"The same thing I always do—you."

"But I'll be in Washington, DC."

"And there's no one who could do a better job. Not even me." And then she blushed.

"What?"

She shook her head, but he waited her out. Miranda could no more stop a thought once she'd had it than she could keep a secret.

"I'd ask one favor, but it's so presumptuous."

"Ask anyway."

"Could you," she blushed brighter, "analyze mine first when I send them in to you? I hate to jump to the front of the line if there are multiple incidents occurring but the timeliness is so critical in many of my investigations and—"

"Anything for you, Miranda."

She looked at him in surprise. "That's the same thing Andi said to me last night. Though her tone seemed rather different."

Jeremy knew that Miranda's ASD would make tone a nuance that she could rarely penetrate. Two years ago, air-crash investigations had been like that to him. Impenetrable. Mysterious. Disorder and chaos at a maximum and explanations only discovered after intensive research. Miranda had taught him how to bring order to the chaos, to find the answers, the *tone* of the accident often leading to the core of the solution.

"How was our tone different?"

"Well..." Miranda inspected the sky, which had a pair of bald eagles circling high above. Then the trees, which had taken over once they reached the north end of the runway. "You simply said it."

"I meant it."

"I know. Or you wouldn't have said it. I believe that Andi meant it too. We were lying together under my sunset quilt at the time. She said it like this," then she leaned close and whispered it so close to his ear that it tickled. "Does that mean it had other implications?"

It didn't take any imagination to picture Taz saying something like that to him in that tone...she'd done something similar any number of times and the results were always—

Now Jeremy could feel the heat rushing to *his* face. How in the world was he going to explain this without crashing and burning?

7

Her kitchen was a disaster. It had been cleaned, at least there was that, which appeared to be Andi's doing. But the spices were no longer sectioned by cuisine, nor were they in any other order that she could ascertain except alphabetic by the third letter—mostly.

The flour was supposed to be organized by color: rice, bread, all-purpose, buckwheat, rye, and whole wheat. Corn flour, being so yellow, had always worried her. She'd finally kept it at the end, but now it sat next to the rice flour, which wasn't even close.

Measuring spoons weren't nested.

They'd used the brownie pan rather than the cake tin and hadn't nested them properly when putting them away.

The mayhem didn't end there either.

While Holly and Andi had baked, Mike and Taz had cooked. Long skewers of beef, chicken strips, and vegetables were arranged in no apparent order. There was scant attention paid to measuring out the spacing and making sure that the opening sequence was repeated down the entire length of the skewer. Peanut sauce for the chicken meant that her peanut butter would be out of place. From-scratch BBQ sauce implied...she shuddered to think about it.

But she had to admit that the party was fun. Holly had womaned the grill. They sat at the big picnic table on the front patio, looking south and west across the mile of blue water separating her home from San Juan Island. Sailboats, power boats, and the occasional large green-and-white car ferries plied the waters.

Tall glasses of strawberry iced tea and chill bottles of beer adorned the well-laden table. They'd eaten and talked through the warm afternoon and well into the cool evening. The breeze had stayed up in the tops of the trees, making the dark green firs wave against the darkening sky, without disturbing their party. Other than bird calls and the now rare boat, the silence wrapped around them with only the waves lapping on the shore offering a constant backdrop of sound. It was one of her favorite times of day.

A few deer visited, but only the youngest doe on the island, Thumper, came forward. Miranda had tucked some dried apple rings in her pocket and fed them to the deer. Then she scritched its back close before the tail. In response, Thumper happily closed her eyes as she chewed and one of her rear legs spasmed in delight, thumping the ground.

She had to walk away from the team to feed the other deer a few apple rings.

By the time she had returned, everything had been

cleared away, creating more disorder in her kitchen she was sure.

Then Holly arrived bearing the cake. It was big enough to serve twenty rather than just the six of them. A blue-and-silver helicopter made out of frosted gingerbread was perched high atop of dowel that had been jammed into the cake. Painted on the windows were six faces. She and Andi at the front, the others equally easy to make out. They all seemed to be looking down at the cake.

The cake itself was blinding. Great swaths of colored fondant and royal icing had been layered over the top. Some neat, some haphazard, showing the effects of multiple hands turned to the task. Without the helicopter as a clue, she might not have been able to make out the decoration, but she soon realized that the bands of colors were tulips. The fields they had flown over only hours before. Two strips were thick with a mixture of every color of sprinkle she owned, where the mixed-color bulbs had been planted. She wondered if she had any sprinkles left. She'd have to add them to the next shopping list.

Over it all, in gigantic green letters, someone had written, *Glad to be rid of you both!*

Holly.

"It's—"

"Stunningly beautiful!" Holly announced. "Even if I do say so myself."

It wasn't, but it was terribly cheerful.

Miranda did her best not to focus on the sadness, that it also depicted what was probably their second-to-last flight together as a team. Tomorrow they would...deal with tomorrow. She couldn't bear to think about it.

After the kitchen had been returned to some kind of order, they had sat in the great room long into the night, not wanting to let go of the moment. The house fell quiet quickly when everyone finally went off to bed.

Thanks to Jeremy, Miranda now understood something she hadn't last night. As she curled up beside Andi in the master bedroom she whispered, "Anything for you, Andi."

It was much closer to dawn before either of them fell asleep.

8

GOODBYES WERE NOT SOMETHING MIRANDA COULD tolerate. They simply hurt too much.

Andi had insisted that she had to join them when they flew back to the Tacoma hangar and they all went to the Gig Harbor team house together the next morning, but even that was difficult.

Jeremy had arranged for a truck, along with a tow trailer for their car. With everyone helping it was soon loaded.

But before the goodbyes could start. Miranda had hugged both Jeremy and Taz quickly, then driven to the hangar office while the others said goodbye at the team house.

While she waited for Andi, she considered flying up to the island on her own, to retreat into the privacy she so often needed to clear her head. But she didn't...want to. The feeling was as elusive as such things always were for her, but when she pictured being alone on her family island, it felt...lonely.

Yet the hangar office felt equally strange. Jeremy's workbench had been organized, everything stowed in its proper place without a single project's paperwork spread out. He'd have far better equipment at NTSB headquarters in DC. Until they arrived there, he still had the contents of his site-investigation field pack. He was always the best-equipped team member during any investigation. She chose to carry the tools she'd found to be essential. He'd made a different choice; Jeremy always carried as much as he physically could.

While waiting alone, though she wasn't sure exactly for what, she prowled the office. Memories lay thick on every surface. Some of them were still here, Holly's favorite spot on the couch, facing the big TV screen. Mike's armchair and the small side table where he often set an espresso and his latest flavor of biscotti.

Andi had left many impressions, the piled pillows at the end of Miranda's favorite couch where she often curled up with a book or technical manual. The small weight set and exercise machine that was as much a part of her soldier's nature as it was Taz and Holly's.

But the lacks, the holes where Taz and Jeremy had been, were aching voids.

In an attempt to calm herself, she finally sat at her desk and propped her feet on the safe.

The safe.

Had Jeremy remembered to take the Black Box reader?

She quickly opened the safe, but the reader was gone.

She slowly extracted the package that was there in its place and set it on the center of her rolltop desk.

Andi came in behind her, wrapped an arm around Miranda's shoulders from behind and kissed her on top of the head.

"I thought you'd be gone. Up to the island."

"I didn't want to go. Not without...you." That's what would have been missing if she'd gone on her own. None of her past relationships would have felt that way, but her one with Andi did. She didn't know why, perhaps she didn't need to, as Andi tightened her hug. It was simply truth, whether or not the reason was hidden from her.

"What's that?" Miranda could feel Andi's nod toward the package on her desk.

"I don't know. I haven't unwrapped it yet."

Andi didn't let go as Miranda did so. She liked the feeling of support, of calm acceptance of whatever came next. Somehow it would be okay.

When the last piece of paper was peeled aside, Andi began to laugh.

Miranda perhaps understood Taz's reaction during the furniture delivery a little better as she herself began to cry.

Jeremy had used cookies and bright orange fondant to make a miniature model of a Black Box recorder. On the side, he'd lettered *The Future*.

And he was right. The future was a mystery, but the answers were there. Inside, hidden for now—but they were there.

She turned enough that she could look up at Andi, "Let's go home."

———

If you enjoyed this story
please consider leaving a review.
They really help.

Keep reading for an exciting excerpt from:
Miranda Chase #10: *Lightning (coming soon)*

LIGHTNING (EXCERPT)

IF YOU ENJOYED THAT, YOU'LL LOVE
THIS COLLECTION!

LIGHTNING (EXCERPT)

MIRANDA CHASE #10

"PULL TO THE CURB HERE!"

CIA Director Clarissa Reese's driver obeyed and slid out of the thick Friday evening traffic pushing into Columbus Circle. The congestion was worse than ever as everyone tried to escape the already sweltering city for the Memorial Day weekend. He eased into a crosswalk at the corner of North Capitol and E Streets, a half-block shy of the George Hotel to her left. In a token gesture to the pedestrians, he backed up three feet to clear a slice of it, as if they mattered.

Behind her, the US Capitol Building glowed orange in the May sunset; the sun still touched the dark bronze Statue of Freedom atop the dome so that it shone brighter than anything else in Washington, DC. Clarissa could feel her baleful glare like a simmering heat at the back of Clarissa's head.

She wished she could light the statue like a fuse on a dome-sized bomb—or at least a missile-sized one shoved up the backsides of each member of the House Permanent Select Committee on Intelligence.

The fact that she knew she was overreacting did little to ease the knot that had built in her stomach throughout today's excruciating meetings, though she'd been careful to keep that off her face. Hadn't she?

Ahead, the columned facade of Union Station, stained dull orange by the setting sun, glowered at her as if daring her to leave town. For the first time in her career, that actually sounded tempting.

She didn't want to face...anything.

"Pull yourself together, Clarissa." Her self-instruction wasn't helping. She'd been muttering some version of it over and over for the last three weeks with minimal effect.

Her driver studiously ignored her. She'd long since made it clear that the last thing she needed was to interact with any agent who'd never be more than a security hack. By the time she was his age, she'd been at a CIA Black Site extracting information from the worst dregs of humanity involved in the Afghan madness.

There'd been an art to that that she'd thoroughly mastered.

This? This was hard. In the last month she'd lost everything.

With her husband's death, her path to the White House had been blocked. Vice Presidents were *supposed* to be well protected. But not Clark. His Marine Two helicopter had gone down in flames, the bastard.

Then, the goddamn President had elevated his

National Security Adviser to become Vice President Sarah Feldman rather than herself.

That had put Clarissa on the street when the new VP moved into the grand Queen Anne Victorian at One Observatory Circle. She never should have sold her prime condo in Foggy Bottom, but Clark had been such an obvious shoo-in to the White House that she'd been assured of her future residence for years to come. At the rate the housing market was exploding here, even the sale of Clark's *country* place out in Nowheresville, Maryland—whoever heard of Poolesville that didn't actually live there—wouldn't make up the difference.

For the moment she had a crap townhouse out in Langley.

And *no* part in the biggest political initiative since Bretton Woods and the Cold War.

The President's new MERP—Middle East Realignment Plan—had captured the imagination of everyone from the unwashed masses to all but the most jaundiced Washington elite. Even marginal allies were flocking to the call.

Worse, President Cole had made sure that the bulk of the credit had gone to the new VP. If the woman didn't screw up, she had the next election, eighteen months out, in the bag.

Of course, when Sarah ran, she *would* need a Vice President...

The hidden scandals—thankfully, all classified top secret but littered with Clarissa's name—had guaranteed her shut-out of any future chance at the Oval Office. It was clear that *certain parties* would release everything if she tried to run. The House Intelligence Committee— that was damn well supposed to be on her side—had made that indisputably clear all through today's meetings.

She had enough dirt to ruin half the committee and have the other half burned at the stake. But their idea of a united front was, if they went down, they'd take her down with them.

Bush's route of CIA Director to Vice President to the Oval was lost to her, and it was time she accepted it. Time to move on...but in what direction?

Clarissa stared at the cubic brick edifice of the George Hotel and did her best to discover some shred of composure. It had become harder and harder in the weeks since Clark's death as she discovered more pieces of herself that she'd lost in addition to her home and her path to the White House, like the surprising revelation that she missed Clark himself. Immensely.

Her fortieth birthday was in three days, and Clark had promised her a big celebration. She'd planned one of herself, announcing her own place as Vice President on his ticket for the next election. But she'd also looked forward to whatever surprise he'd had planned. But the surprise of his unrevealed plan had followed him to the grave.

Even in death he wouldn't leave her alone.

The other thing today's meetings in those hallowed corridors of cold stone beneath the Capitol Dome had proven was that, for once, she'd misjudged the power plays completely. It wasn't something she didn't very often—and never before so badly.

At the White House's request, she'd drawn up a master list of every known terrorist action against the US. She'd done so for every nation from Afghanistan to Zimbabwe—actually to Yemen as both Zambia and Zimbabwe were too busy wallowing in their own shit to bother the US in any notable way.

And she'd listed every CIA counterstroke, the good and the bad. She'd left out the true Black Ops performed by the Special Operations Group and anything that was patently illegal, but included everything else.

It was supposed to be a strictly internal document, but it had predictably leaked. Clarissa had expected that and planned accordingly. The disastrous 1974 leak of the dreaded *Family Jewels* memos had chronicled hundreds of times that the CIA had overstepped their charter. The public and Congressional retribution, which had nearly led to the breakup of the CIA, were not going to happen on her watch.

And they hadn't.

Instead, against all projections, the opposite had occurred.

Clarissa had carefully laid all of the questionable activities at Clark's feet as he'd been the CIA Director before her. Finally, having a dead Vice President for a predecessor and a husband came in handy.

It was always better when they blamed a dead man.

Except, instead of the leaked summary wreaking domestic havoc this time, it had become a key document in the President's proposed MERP. It had justified massive realignments and the disavowal of several long-term Middle East allies with their fingers deep in terrorism.

Rather than shaking the nation, it had inspired it.

It had also elevated Clark's posthumous popularity far past anything it deserved. She knew that for a fact as she'd spent years engineering his image during his ascendency. Now it was impossible to take back the credit, even for her own operations, that she had so publicly given away. The House Intelligence Committee had made that abundantly clear this afternoon.

This committee will protect our nation and Vice President Clark Winston's legacy—despite knowing damn well how much of that was hers—*against all comers.* The silence that followed had echoed about the meeting room until it hurt her ears. They'd *gladly* shred her reputation, if they thought they could survive doing so themselves.

Clarissa sighed. Grinding on past woes would achieve nothing. She needed a way ahead. The committee had kept her until she was late for her monthly dinner meeting with Senator Hunter and Rose Ramson in The George's penthouse suite.

She didn't need the influence of the Chairman of the Senate Armed Service Committee. Hunter had lost much of his power in his efforts to block the President's Middle East Realignment Plan. MERP had voided billions of dollars of foreign arms sales for Hunter's pet defense contractors and dropped his lobbying power to near zero.

To say that the contractors and the Saudis, among

others, were livid about his inability to quash MERP was a significant understatement. They'd all become much less friendly over these same three weeks since Clark's death.

No, she hadn't needed anything from Hunter since his fall from grace. There was even growing doubt regarding his retention of his seat in the Senate for a fifth six-year term at the next election. There were rumors—that she knew to be true—that *both* parties were vetting new candidates to replace the suddenly vulnerable Hunter Ramson. No longer the favored son.

What Clarissa needed tonight was the sharp mind of Washington's top socialite, Rose Ramson, *The First Lady of DC.* Perhaps so powerful on her own that she could weather the storm of her husband's fall.

Clarissa had once promised Rose the future Vice Presidency but, as hard as it was to accept, that was gone and they both knew it. The question now was, could Rose help her consolidate what power she did have? Clarissa would leave it up to Rose to name her price.

Sadly, Clarissa suspected that her scattered thoughts wouldn't become any more coherent than they were at this moment.

"Let's get this done already," she finally told the driver.

Pedestrians had stopped in the narrow slice of crosswalk at the front of the car. They were gawking and pointing at something behind her.

The driver checked his side mirror—ducking low to look upward. He didn't look away.

Clarissa turned to look out the rear window.

Instead of a big truck blocking the lane, she spotted a jet, a black blot on an achingly deep blue evening sky. Weaving around the Capitol Dome like the Statue of Freedom was the marker post for turn Number Four in a horse race, it sped toward them—where no planes were ever supposed to be.

Downtown DC was the most protected no-fly zone in the country.

An idiot, hoping to be in tomorrow's headlines for buzzing DC, had swooped between the Capitol and the Supreme Court Building, and was now carving a hard turn at Columbus Circle above Union Station.

Heading for the White House? If both Cole and Feldman were there, and it all went wrong... But the Speaker of the House, next in line, was a ridiculous progressive and had no love for the CIA, making him hard to leverage.

It was a sleek C-21A Learjet painted US Air Force blah.

"Damn, they're low," her driver spoke for the first time since leaving the Capitol Building.

They were.

In fact, they were so low that—

The plane passed close overhead as it flew into the narrow slot of E Street Northwest, which was barely wider than its wingspan.

Below the tops of the buildings.

The sonic lash of its jet engines reverberated along the brick-and-glass canyon. The wind of its passage slammed into them hard enough to shake her Cadillac Escalade SUV despite the extra weight of the Class VI up-armor and thick bullet-proof glass.

Rather than racing along E Street for the mile and a half to the White House, the jet banked right with an abrupt twist—and flew into the side of a building.

The moment was so unreal she couldn't blink or turn away. It looked like a Hollywood film without any slo-mo or alternate angle shots.

The plane disappeared through the wall of the top floor.

For a moment…nothing.

Only a dark hole where the outer windows and red brick no longer reflected the sunset sky.

Then a fireball roiled out in a massive plume.

Two seconds later, all of the glass and much of the brick on that floor blew outward as the plane exploded deep inside the building.

Half a block away, the shock wave slammed her SUV hard enough that the shoulder belt was all that kept her in her seat.

A cloud of debris rained down on the heavy traffic. Her car rattled in the massive hailstorm of debris peppering the body. A block of bricks the size of a footstool slammed off the center of the hood with a bang of bending steel louder than a gunshot, making both her and the driver jump. It tumbled into the crowd of gawking pedestrians.

Screams of the injured added to the mayhem of car alarms and blasting horns. The hard crunch of fender benders as drivers lost control. The cries when they crushed an unwary pedestrian in the process.

While the last of the debris still pattered down upon them—a pair of *alert* fighter jets raced low over the city. Not a sonic boom, but so loud that Clarissa ducked despite knowing they were far above her and in better control than the first jet had been. They disappeared to the west, circled hard, and made another roaring pass over the unfolding disaster.

Too little, too late.

When she looked up again, she finally noticed which building had been struck.

It was The George Hotel.

The top floor.

The point of entry...

The southeast corner suite—

Clarissa barely flinched as a car slammed into her passenger door. Numb with shock, she couldn't move a single muscle.

She was used to looking *out* that window, not locating it from the outside.

The Learjet *hadn't* been out of control.

It had impacted the hotel *precisely* where, at this very moment, she was supposed to be having her monthly dinner with the Ramsons. The couple stayed there on the last Friday of every month to enjoy the Presidential Suite's luxury—or rather the luxury of its bed—proceeded by a fine dinner and an off-the-books meeting with Clarissa, the Director of the CIA.

Either the defense contractors or the Saudis had tired of Senator Ramson failing them.

Or both.

Or, Clarissa couldn't swallow against a throat gone dry, had the House Intelligence Committee decided it was time to erase her?

———

Coming soon!

ABOUT THE AUTHOR

USA Today and Amazon #1 Bestseller M. L. "Matt" Buchman has 70+ action-adventure thriller and military romance novels, 100 short stories, and lotsa audiobooks. PW says: "Tom Clancy fans open to a strong female lead will clamor for more." Booklist declared: "3X Top 10 of the Year." A project manager with a geophysics degree, he's designed and built houses, flown and jumped out of planes, solo-sailed a 50' sailboat, and bicycled solo around the world...and he quilts. More at: www.mlbuchman.com.

Other works by M. L. Buchman: (* - also in audio)

Action-Adventure Thrillers

Dead Chef
One Chef!
Two Chef!

Miranda Chase
Drone*
Thunderbolt*
Condor*
Ghostrider*
Raider*
Chinook*
Havoc*
White Top*
Start the Chase*

Science Fiction / Fantasy

Deities Anonymous
Cookbook from Hell: Reheated
Saviors 101

Single Titles
Monk's Maze
the Me and Elsie Chronicles

Contemporary Romance

Eagle Cove
Return to Eagle Cove
Recipe for Eagle Cove
Longing for Eagle Cove
Keepsake for Eagle Cove

Love Abroad
Heart of the Cotswolds: England
Path of Love: Cinque Terre, Italy

Where Dreams
Where Dreams are Born
Where Dreams Reside
Where Dreams Are of Christmas*
Where Dreams Unfold
Where Dreams Are Written
Where Dreams Continue

Non-Fiction

Strategies for Success
Managing Your Inner Artist/Writer
Estate Planning for Authors*
Character Voice
Narrate and Record Your Own
Audiobook*

Short Story Series by M. L. Buchman:

Action-Adventure Thrillers

Dead Chef

Miranda Chase Origin Stories

Romantic Suspense

Antarctic Ice Fliers

US Coast Guard

Contemporary Romance

Eagle Cove

Other

Deities Anonymous (fantasy)

Single Titles

The Emily Beale Universe
(military romantic suspense)

The Night Stalkers
MAIN FLIGHT
The Night Is Mine
I Own the Dawn
Wait Until Dark
Take Over at Midnight
Light Up the Night
Bring On the Dusk
By Break of Day
Target of the Heart
Target Lock on Love
Target of Mine
Target of One's Own
NIGHT STALKERS HOLIDAYS
*Daniel's Christmas**
*Frank's Independence Day**
*Peter's Christmas**
Christmas at Steel Beach
*Zachary's Christmas**
*Roy's Independence Day**
*Damien's Christmas**
Christmas at Peleliu Cove

Henderson's Ranch
*Nathan's Big Sky**
*Big Sky, Loyal Heart**
*Big Sky Dog Whisperer**
*Tales of Henderson's Ranch**

Shadow Force: Psi
*At the Slightest Sound**
*At the Quietest Word**
*At the Merest Glance**
*At the Clearest Sensation**

White House Protection Force
*Off the Leash**
*On Your Mark**
*In the Weeds**

Firehawks
Pure Heat
Full Blaze
*Hot Point**
*Flash of Fire**
Wild Fire
SMOKEJUMPERS
*Wildfire at Dawn**
*Wildfire at Larch Creek**
*Wildfire on the Skagit**

Delta Force
*Target Engaged**
*Heart Strike**
*Wild Justice**
*Midnight Trust**

Emily Beale Universe Short Story Series

The Night Stalkers
The Night Stalkers Stories
The Night Stalkers CSAR
The Night Stalkers Wedding Stories
The Future Night Stalkers

Delta Force
Th Delta Force Shooters
The Delta Force Warriors

Firehawks
The Firehawks Lookouts
The Firehawks Hotshots
The Firebirds

White House Protection Force
Stories

Future Night Stalkers
Stories (Science Fiction)

SIGN UP FOR M. L. BUCHMAN'S NEWSLETTER TODAY

and receive:
Release News
Free Short Stories
a Free Book

Get your free book today. Do it now.
free-book.mlbuchman.com

Printed in Great Britain
by Amazon